Leo Lionni Favorites:
Six Classic Stories

Leo Lionni
Favorites:
Six Classic
Stories

Alfred A. Knopf New York

Contents

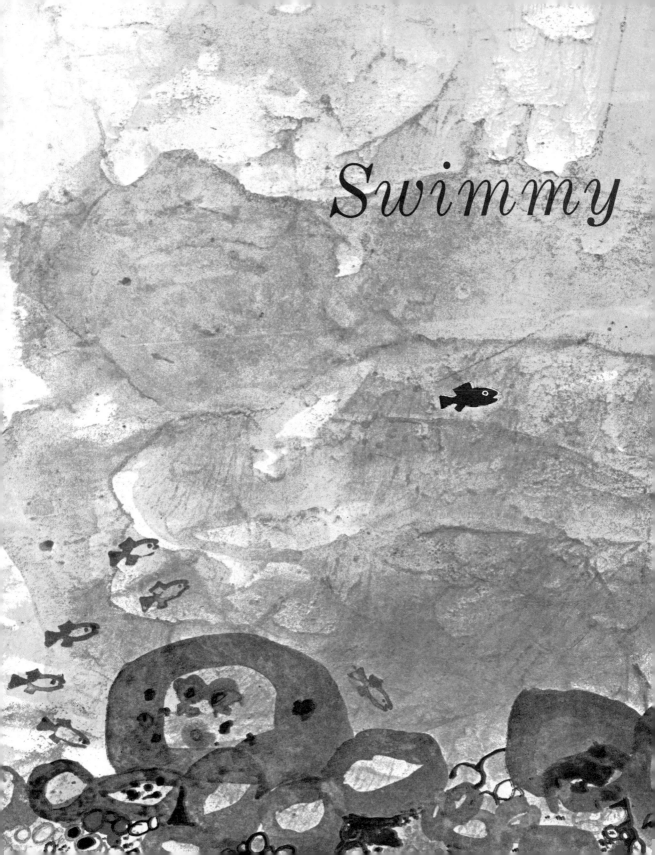

Swimmy

A happy school of little fish lived in a corner of the sea somewhere.
They were all red. Only one of them was as black as a mussel shell.
He swam faster than his brothers and sisters. His name was Swimmy.

One bad day a tuna fish, swift, fierce and very hungry, came darting through the waves. In one gulp he swallowed all the little red fish. Only Swimmy escaped.

He swam away in the deep wet world. He was scared, lonely and very sad.

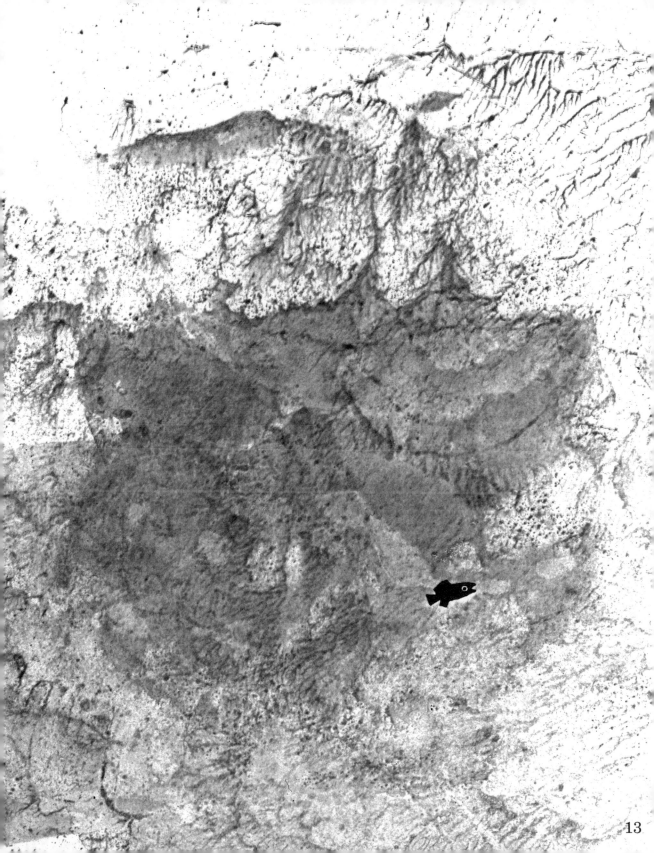

13

But the sea was full of wonderful creatures, and as he swam from marvel to marvel Swimmy was happy again.

He saw a medusa made of rainbow jelly...

a lobster, who walked about like a water-moving machine...

strange fish, pulled by an invisible thread...

a forest of seaweeds growing from sugar-candy rocks…

an eel whose tail was almost too far away to remember...

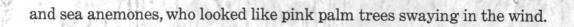

and sea anemones, who looked like pink palm trees swaying in the wind.

Then, hidden in the dark shade of rocks and weeds, he saw a school of little fish, just like his own.

"Let's go and swim and play and SEE things!" he said happily.
"We can't," said the little red fish. "The big fish will eat us all."

"But you can't just lie there," said Swimmy. "We must THINK of something."

Swimmy thought and thought and thought.

Then suddenly he said, "I have it!"
"We are going to swim all together like the biggest fish in the sea!"

He taught them to swim close together, each in his own place,

and when they had learned to swim like one giant fish, he said, "I'll be the eye."

And so they swam in the cool morning water and in the midday sun and

chased the big fish away.

TICO
and the golden wings

Many years ago
I knew a little bird
whose name was Tico.
He would sit on my shoulder
and tell me all about the flowers,
the ferns, and the tall trees.
Once Tico told me
this story about himself.

I don't know how it happened,
but when I was young
I had no wings.
I sang like the other birds
and I hopped like them,
but I couldn't fly.

Luckily my friends loved me. They flew from tree to tree and in the evening they brought me berries and tender fruits gathered from the highest branches.

Often I asked myself, "Why can't I fly like the other birds? Why can't I, too, soar through the big blue sky over villages and treetops?"

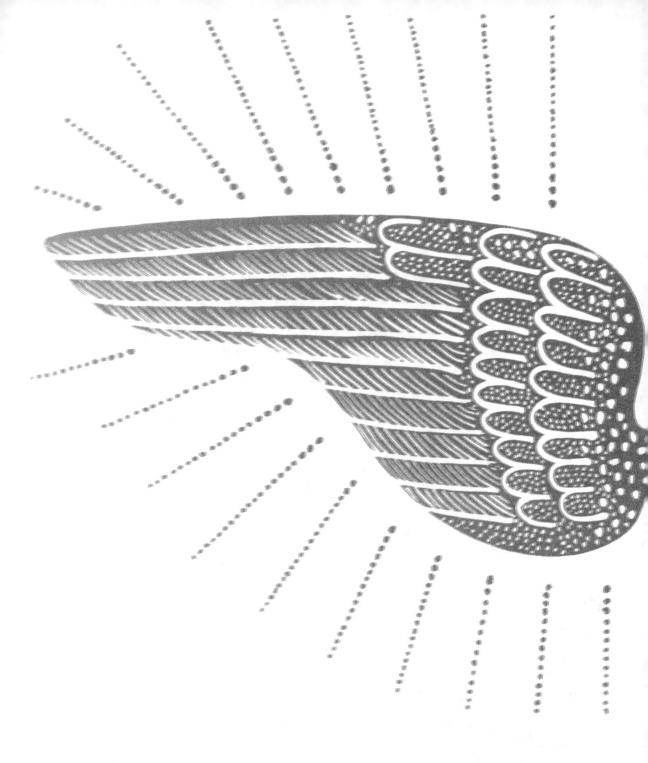

And I dreamt that I had golden wings, strong enough

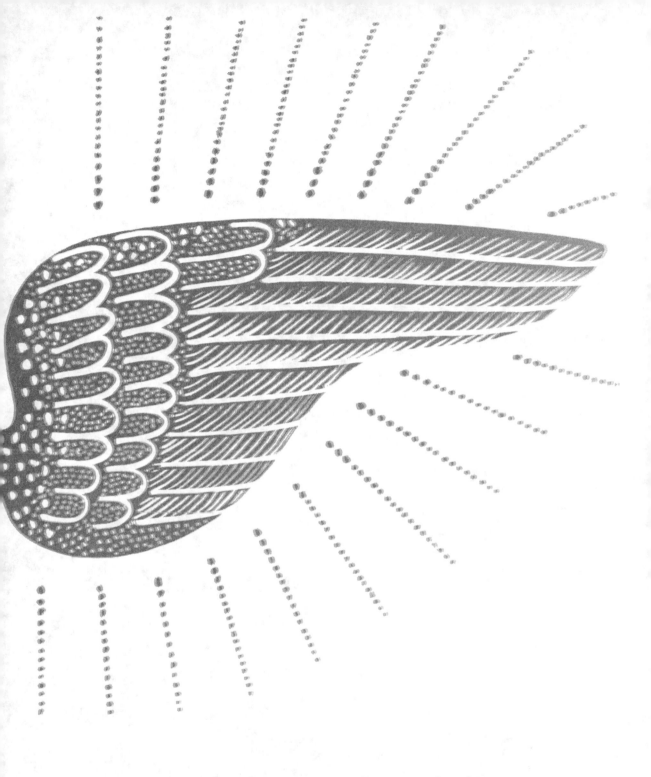

to carry me over the snowcapped mountains far away.

One summer night I was awakened by a noise near by. A strange bird, pale as a pearl, was standing behind me.
"I am the wishingbird," he said. "Make a wish and it will come true."

I remembered my dreams and with all my might I wished I had a pair of golden wings. Suddenly there was a flash of light and on my back there were wings, golden wings, shimmering in the moonlight. The wishingbird had vanished.

Cautiously I flapped my wings. And then I flew.
I flew higher than the tallest tree. The flower patches below
looked like stamps scattered over the countryside
and the river like a silver necklace lying in the meadows.
I was happy and I flew well into the day.

But when my friends saw me
swoop down from the sky,
they frowned on me and said,
"You think you are better than we are,
don't you, with those golden wings.
You wanted to be *different*."
And off they flew
without saying another word.

Why had they gone? Why were they angry?
Was it *bad* to be different?
I could fly as high as the eagle.
Mine were the most beautiful wings in the world.
But my friends had left me and I was very lonely.

51

One day I saw a man sitting
in front of a hut.
He was a basketmaker
and there were baskets
all around him.
There were tears in his eyes.
I flew onto a branch from
where I could speak to him.

"Why are you sad?" I asked.
"Oh, little bird, my child is sick
and I am poor.
I cannot buy the medicines
that would make him well."
"How can I help him?" I thought.
And suddenly I knew.
"I will give him one of my feathers

"How can I thank you!" said the poor man happily.
"You have saved my child. But look! Your wing!"
Where the golden feather had been
there was a real black feather, as soft as silk.

From that day, little by little,
I gave my golden feathers away
and black feathers appeared in their place.
I bought many presents:
three new puppets for a poor puppeteer . . .

57

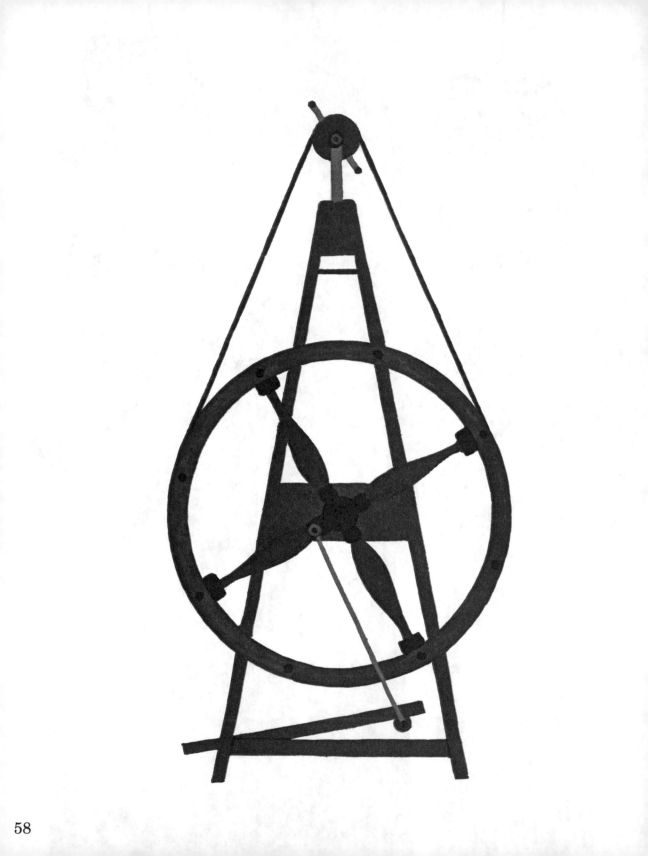

a spinning wheel to spin the yarn for an old woman's shawl . . .

a compass for a fisherman who got lost at sea . . .

And when I had given my last golden feathers
to a beautiful bride,
my wings were as black as India ink.

61

I flew to the big tree
where my friends gathered for the night.
Would they welcome me?

They chirped with joy.
"Now you are just like us," they said.
We all huddled close together.
But I was so happy and excited
I couldn't sleep.
I remembered the basketmaker's son,
the old woman, the puppeteer,
and all the others I had helped
with my feathers.
"Now my wings are black," I thought,
"and yet I am not like my friends.
We are *all* different.
Each for his own memories,
and his own invisible golden dreams."

Fish
is
Fish

At the edge of the woods there was a pond, and there a minnow
and a tadpole swam among the weeds. They were inseparable
friends.

One morning the tadpole discovered that during the night he had grown two little legs.

"Look" he said triumphantly. "Look, I am a frog!"

"Nonsense," said the minnow. "How could you be a frog if only last night you were a little fish, just like me!"

They argued and argued until finally the tadpole said, "Frogs are frogs and fish is fish and that's that!"

In the weeks that followed, the tadpole grew tiny front legs and his tail got smaller and smaller.

And then one fine day, a real frog now, he climbed out of the water and onto the grassy bank.

The minnow too had grown and had become a full-fledged fish. He often wondered where his four-footed friend had gone. But days and weeks went by and the frog did not return.

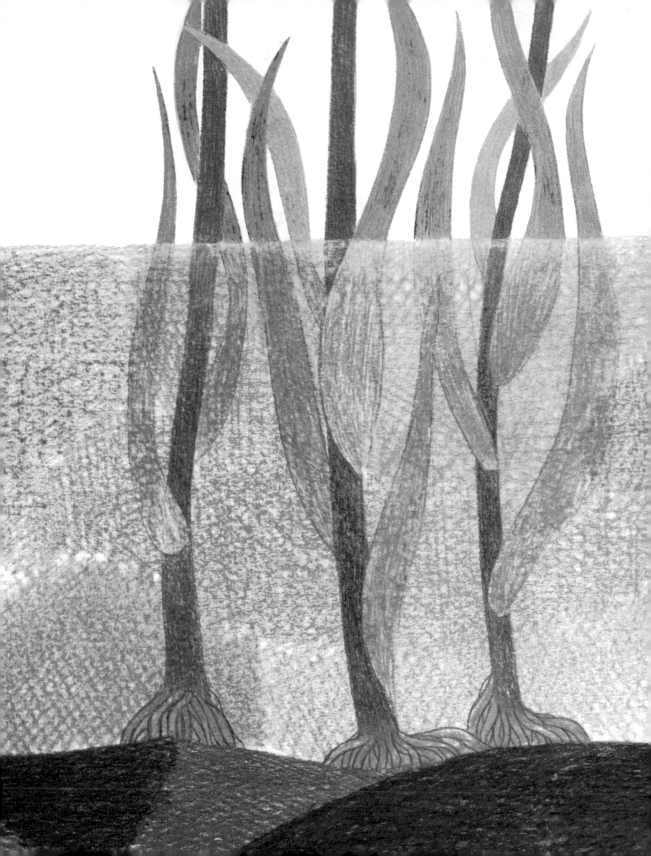

Then one day, with a happy splash that shook the weeds, the frog jumped into the pond.

"Where have you been?" asked the fish excitedly.

"I have been about the world—hopping here and there," said the frog, "and I have seen extraordinary things."

"Like what?" asked the fish.

"Birds," said the frog mysteriously. "Birds!" And he told the fish about the birds, who had wings, and two legs, and many, many colors.

As the frog talked, his friend saw the birds fly through his mind like large feathered fish.

"What else?" asked the fish impatiently.

"Cows," said the frog. "Cows! They have four legs, horns, eat grass, and carry pink bags of milk."

"And people!" said the frog. "Men, women, children!" And he talked and talked until it was dark in the pond.

But the picture in the fish's mind was full of lights and colors and marvelous things and he couldn't sleep. Ah, if he could only jump about like his friend and see that wonderful world.

And so the days went by. The frog had gone and the fish just lay there dreaming about birds in flight, grazing cows, and those strange animals, all dressed up, that his friend called people.

One day he finally decided that come what may, he too must see them. And so with a mighty whack of the tail he jumped clear out of the water onto the bank.

He landed in the dry, warm grass and there he lay gasping for air, unable to breathe or to move. "Help," he groaned feebly.

Luckily the frog, who had been hunting butterflies nearby, saw him and with all his strength pushed him back into the pond.

93

Still stunned, the fish floated about for an instant. Then he breathed deeply, letting the clean cool water run through his gills. Now he felt weightless again and with an ever-so-slight motion of the tail he could move to and fro, up and down, as before.

The sunrays reached down within the weeds and gently shifted patches of luminous color. This world was surely the most beautiful of all worlds. He smiled at his friend the frog, who sat watching him from a lily leaf. "You were right," he said. "Fish is fish."

Alexander and the Wind-Up Mouse

"Help! Help! A mouse!" There was a scream. Then a crash.
Cups, saucers, and spoons were flying in all directions.

Alexander ran for his hole as fast as his little legs would carry him.

All Alexander wanted was a few crumbs and yet
every time they saw him they would scream for help
or chase him with a broom.

One day, when there was no one in the house, Alexander heard a squeak in Annie's room. He sneaked in and what did he see? Another mouse.
But not an ordinary mouse like himself. Instead of legs it had two little wheels, and on its back there was a key.

"Who are you?" asked Alexander.

103

"I am Willy the wind-up mouse, Annie's favorite toy. They wind me to make me run around in circles, they cuddle me, and at night I sleep on a soft white pillow between the doll and a woolly teddy bear. Everyone loves me."

"They don't care much for me," said Alexander sadly. But he was happy to have found a friend. "Let's go to the kitchen and look for crumbs," he said.

"Oh, I can't," said Willy. "I can only move when they wind me. But I don't mind. Everybody loves me."

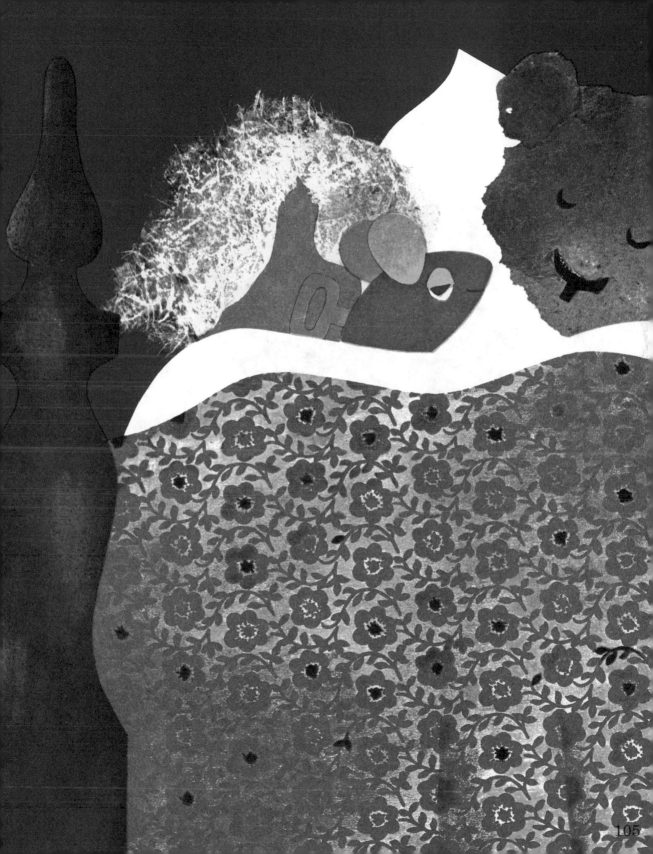

105

106

Alexander, too, came to love Willy. He went to visit him whenever he could. He told him of his adventures with brooms, flying saucers, and mousetraps. Willy talked about the penguin, the woolly bear, and mostly about Annie. The two friends spent many happy hours together.

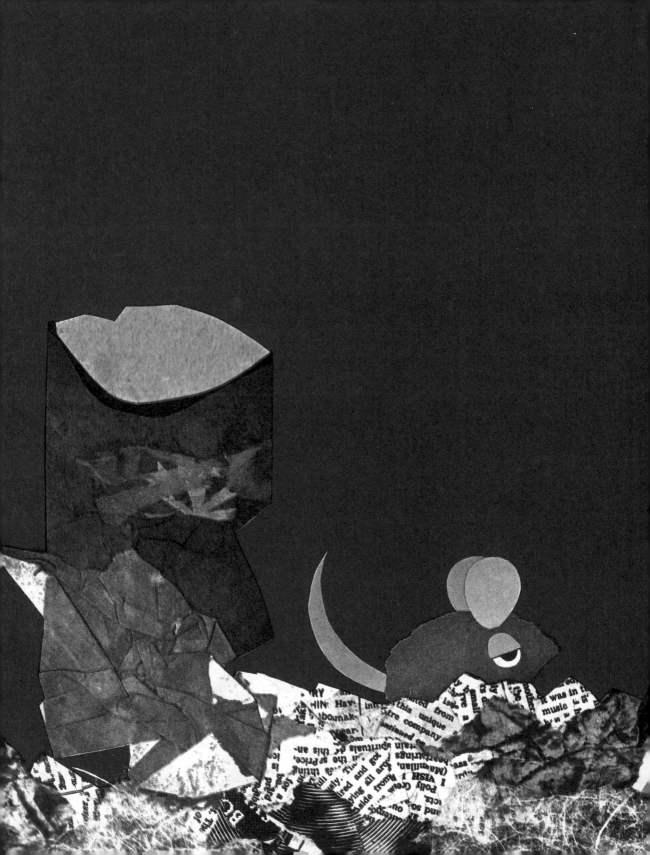

But when he was alone
in the dark of his hideout,
Alexander thought of Willy
with envy.
"Ah!" he sighed. "Why
can't I be a wind-up
mouse like Willy
and be cuddled and loved."

One day Willy told a strange story. "I've heard," he whispered mysteriously, "that in the garden, at the end of the pebblepath, close to the blackberry bush, there lives a magic lizard who can change one animal into another."

"Do you mean," said Alexander, "that he could change me into a wind-up mouse like you?"

That very afternoon Alexander went into the garden and ran to the end of the path. "Lizard, lizard," he whispered. And suddenly there stood before him, full of the colors of flowers and butterflies, a large lizard. "Is it true that you could change me into a wind-up mouse?" asked Alexander in a quivering voice.

"When the moon is round," said the lizard, "bring me a purple pebble."

For days and days Alexander searched the garden for a purple pebble. In vain. He found yellow pebbles and blue pebbles and green pebbles—but not one tiny purple pebble.

At last, tired and hungry, he returned to the
house. In a corner of the pantry he saw a box full of
old toys, and there, between blocks and broken dolls,
was Willy. "What happened?" said Alexander, surprised.

Willy told him a sad story. It had been Annie's birthday.
There had been a party and everyone had brought a gift.
"The next day," Willy sighed, "many of the old toys were
dumped in this box. We will all be thrown away."

Alexander was almost in tears. "Poor,
poor Willy!" he thought. But then
suddenly something caught his eye.
Could it really be ...? Yes it was!
It was a little purple pebble.

117

All excited, he ran to the garden, the precious
pebble tight in his arms. There was a full moon.
Out of breath, Alexander stopped near the
blackberry bush. "Lizard, lizard, in the bush,"
he called quickly. The leaves rustled and
there stood the lizard. "The moon is round,
the pebble found," said the lizard. "Who or
what do you wish to be?"

"I want to be . . ." Alexander stopped.
Then suddenly he said, "Lizard, lizard,
could you change Willy into a mouse like me?"
The lizard blinked. There was a blinding
light. And then all was quiet. The purple pebble
was gone.

Alexander ran back to the house as fast as he could.

The box was there, but alas it was empty. "Too late," he thought, and with a heavy heart he went to his hole in the baseboard.

Something squeaked! Cautiously Alexander moved closer to the hole. There was a mouse inside. "Who are you?" said Alexander, a little frightened.

"My name is Willy," said the mouse.

"Willy!" cried Alexander. "The lizard . . . the lizard did it!"
He hugged Willy and then they ran to the garden path.
And there they danced until dawn.

The Biggest House in the World

Some snails lived on a juicy cabbage.
They moved gently around, carrying their houses
from leaf to leaf, in search of
a tender spot to nibble on.

One day a little snail said to his father,
"When I grow up I want to have the biggest house in the world."
"That is silly," said his father,
who happened to be the wisest snail on the cabbage.
"Some things are better small."
And he told this story.

Once upon a time, a little snail, just like you,
said to his father, "When I grow up
I want to have the biggest house in the world."
"Some things are better small," said his father.
"Keep your house light and easy to carry."

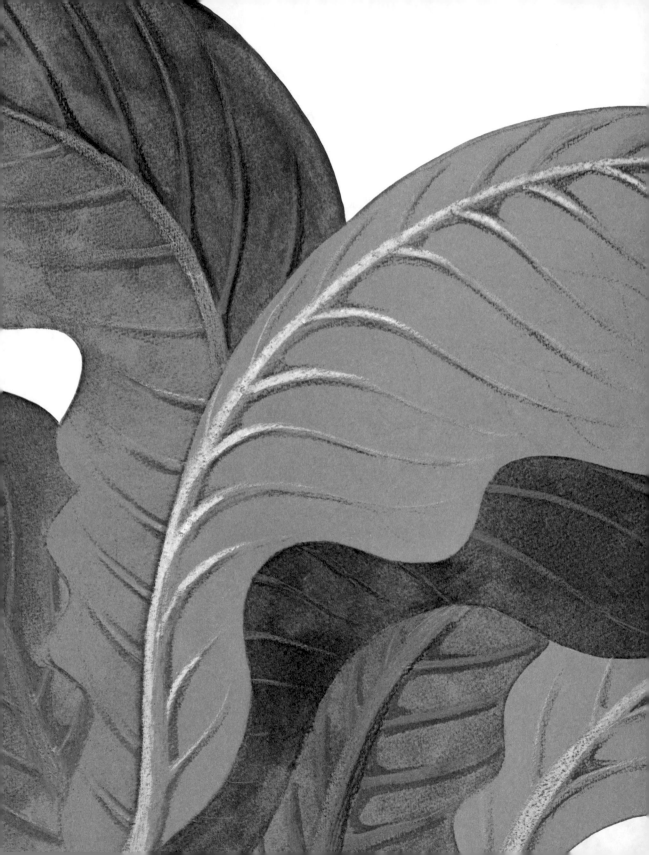

But the little snail would not listen, and
hidden in the shade of a large cabbage leaf, he twisted and twitched,
this way and that, until he discovered how to make his house grow.

It grew and grew, and the snails on the cabbage said,
"You surely have the biggest house in the world."

*The little snail kept on twisting and twitching
until his house was as big as a melon.*

Then, by moving his tail swiftly from left to right,
he learned to grow large pointed bulges.

And by squeezing and pushing, and by wishing very hard,
he was able to add bright colors
and beautiful designs.

Now he knew that his was the biggest and the most beautiful house in the whole world. He was proud and happy.

A swarm of butterflies flew overhead.
"Look!" one of them said. "A cathedral!"
"No," said another, "it's a circus!"
They never guessed that what they were looking at
was the house of a snail.

And a family of frogs, on their way to a distant pond,
stopped in awe. "Never," they later told some cousins,
"never have you seen such an amazing sight.
An ordinary little snail with a house like a birthday cake."

One day after they had eaten all the leaves
and only a few knobby stems were left,
the snails moved to another cabbage.
But the little snail, alas, couldn't move.
His house was much too heavy.

He was left behind, and with nothing to eat
he slowly faded away. Nothing remained but the house.
And that too, little by little, crumbled,
until nothing remained at all.

That was the end of the story. The little snail was almost in tears.

But then he remembered his own house.
"I shall keep it small," he thought,
"and when I grow up I shall go wherever I please."

And so one day, light and joyous, he went on to see the world.
Some leaves fluttered lightly in the breeze,
and others hung heavily to the ground.
Where the dark earth had split, crystals glittered in
the early sun. There were polka-dotted mushrooms,
and towery stems from which little flowers seemed to wave.
There was a pinecone lying in the lacy shade of ferns,
and pebbles in a nest of sand, smooth and round
like the eggs of the turtledove. Lichen clung
to the rocks and bark to the trees.
The tender buds were sweet and cool with morning dew.
The little snail was very happy.

153

The seasons came and went,
but the snail never forgot the story his father had told him.
And when someone asked, "How come you have such a small house?"
he would tell the story of
the biggest house in the world.

Frederick

All along the meadow where the cows grazed and the horses ran, there was an old stone wall.

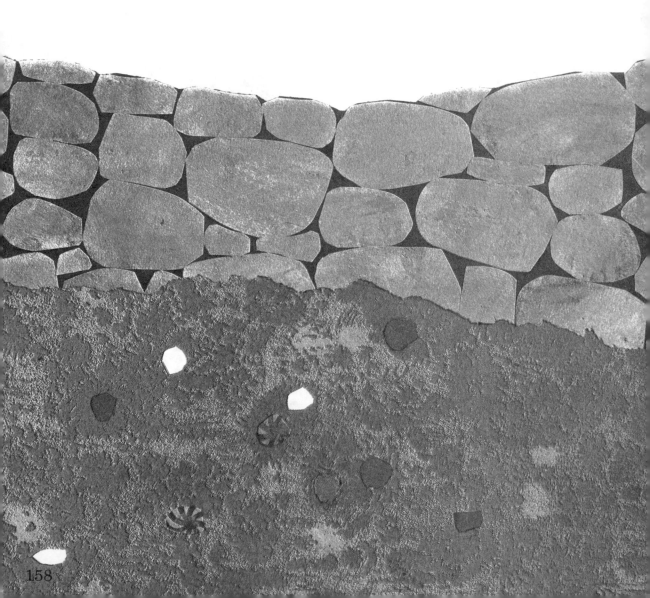

159

In that wall, not far from the barn and the granary,
a chatty family of field mice had their home.

But the farmers had moved away, the barn was abandoned, and the granary stood empty. And since winter was not far off, the little mice began to gather corn and nuts and wheat and straw. They all worked day and night.
All — except Frederick.

163

"Frederick, why don't you work?" they asked.

"I *do* work," said Frederick.

"I gather sun rays for the cold dark winter days."

And when they saw Frederick sitting there, staring at the meadow, they said, "And now, Frederick?" "I gather colors," answered Frederick simply. "For winter is gray."

167

And once Frederick seemed half asleep. "Are you dreaming, Frederick?" they asked reproachfully. But Frederick said, "Oh no, I am gathering words.
For the winter days are long and many,
and we'll run out of things to say."

The winter days came, and when the first snow fell
the five little field mice took to their hideout in the stones.

In the beginning there was lots to eat,
and the mice told stories of foolish foxes
and silly cats. They were a happy family.

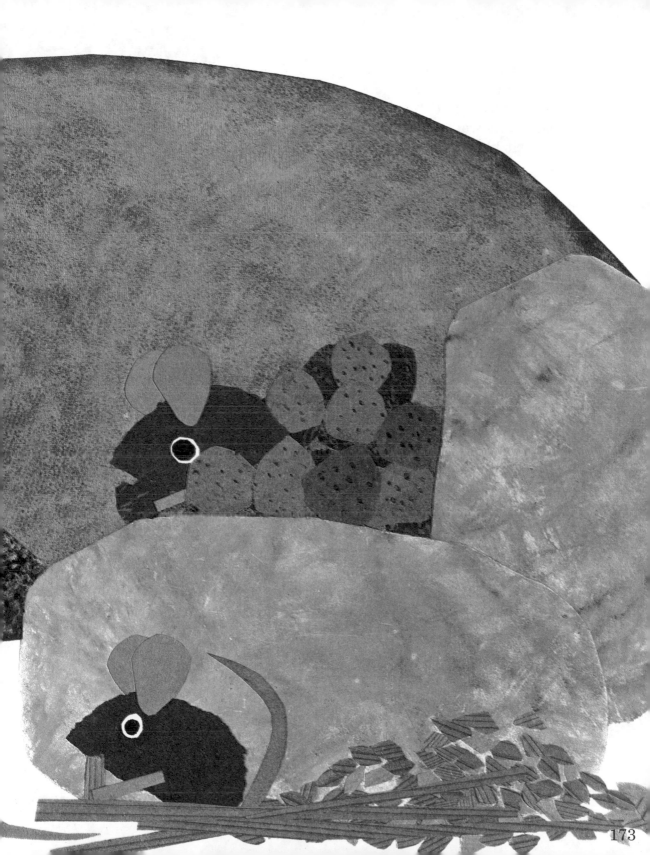

173

But little by little they had nibbled up
most of the nuts and berries, the straw was
gone, and the corn was only a memory.
It was cold in the wall
and no one felt like chatting.

Then they remembered
what Frederick had said about sun rays
and colors and words.
"What about *your* supplies, Frederick?"
they asked.

"Close your eyes," said Frederick,
as he climbed on a big stone.
"Now I send you the rays of the sun.
Do you feel how their golden glow..."
And as Frederick spoke of the sun
the four little mice
began to feel warmer.
Was it Frederick's voice?
Was it magic?

"And how about the colors, Frederick?"
they asked anxiously. "Close your eyes again,"
Frederick said. And when he told them
of the blue periwinkles,
the red poppies in the yellow wheat,
and the green leaves
of the berry bush,
they saw the colors as clearly
as if they had been painted
in their minds.

"And the words, Frederick?"

Frederick cleared his throat,
waited a moment, and then,
as if from a stage, he said:

When Frederick had finished,

"Who scatters snowflakes? Who melts the ice?
Who spoils the weather? Who makes it nice?
Who grows the four-leaf clovers in June?
Who dims the daylight? Who lights the moon?

Four little field mice who live in the sky.
Four little field mice ... like you and I.

One is the Springmouse who turns on the showers.
Then comes the Summer who paints in the flowers.
The Fallmouse is next with walnuts and wheat.
And Winter is last ... with little cold feet.

Aren't we lucky the seasons are four?
Think of a year with one less ... or one more!"

they all applauded. "But Frederick," they said, "you are a poet!"

Frederick blushed, took a bow, and said shyly, "I know it."